I0670543

TRUTH SERUM PRESS

TRUE

TRUTH SERUM
Volume #1

First published February 2017

Content copyright © Truth Serum Press and individual authors
Edited by Matt Potter

All rights reserved by the authors and publisher. Except for brief
excerpts used for review or scholarly purposes, no part of this book
may be reproduced in any manner whatsoever without express
written consent of the publisher or the author/s.

Truth Serum Press
4 Warburton Street
Magill SA 5072
Australia

Email: truthserumpress@live.com.au
Website: http://truthserumpress.net
Truth Serum Press catalogue: http://truthserumpress.net/catalogue/

Original front cover photo *archive folders 5* by Rui Rodrigues
Cover design by Matt Potter

ISBN: 978-1-925536-29-4

Also available as an eBook
ISBN: 978-1-925536-30-0

A note on differences in punctuation and spelling

Truth Serum Press proudly features writers from all over the English-speaking
world. Some speak and write English as their first language, while for others,
it's their second or third or even fourth language. Naturally, across all
versions of English, there are differences in punctuation and spelling, and
even in meaning. These differences are reflected in the work *Truth Serum
Press* publishes, and it accounts for any differences in punctuation, spelling
and meaning found within these pages.

TABLE OF
CONTENTS

A FAIR DINKUM CHAMPION

by

MERCEDES WEBB-PULLMAN

Working in the radio room
sending out price changes on local races
I overhear Gloria and The Prof mention
John the Job so I earwig. He's a mate
I haven't seen lately, but I hear he bred
a dog, trained it himself, and started winning.

'Yes,' says Gloria. 'He lost his home, his
car, then his missus left him. After
his greyhound won the big race.'

We're astonished. You cop it sweet,
losing everything when you're on a bad streak,
but when you're winning? Doesn't make sense.

Gloria settles in, lights up.
She enjoys a good yarn, if it's
someone else's bummer.

'He loved that dog. Spoiled rotten
it was. He treated it like one of his
grandkids: special diets, massages,
even let it sleep on his bed before a race.
Took it to the track in the back of his car,
not in a box. A boof-headed dog who ran
like the power of piss.

The dog was just too good. Bookies
never set a decent price on it; when
it should be six to four, they offered
sixes on. Instead of $660 to win
$1000, it cost him $6000. And still
the dog won. Always at a short price.

Then a bookie talked him into a rort.
Run it dead, fix it so the dog can't win
and share the cash bet on him
as favourite.

They decided on the race. Then John
starved his dog, exhausted it, swam it,
and ran it on sand a bit more. Too tired
to win, and no trace of drugs in its blood.
On the night, the bookie laid it from here
to the black stump, at a point over.
The money poured in.

They stood to lose a fortune if the dog
got up. And of course it did. He'd bred
a fair dinkum champion.

John the Job couldn't get his head around it.
He owed the bookie all he owned. His dog
frisked around, wanting its usual winning
pats and treats. He took it back to his car
and there on the floor he found
a candy-bar wrapper.
A grandkid must have dropped one
and the dog ate it on the way to the track.'
She pauses, sips bourbon.

Bruce, impatient: 'What did he do? What?'
Gloria smiles. It's like seeing lips on a shark.

'He drove out to Wakehurst Parkway and shot it.'

BINOCULARS
(A FOUND POEM)

by

MARK HUDSON

I was in my portraiture class on Saturday, and
some painter had a set of binoculars for
observing close-up details. This was right
before the Thanksgiving break.

"Here," he said to a woman, "You
can borrow these binoculars. I'm going on
a two-week vacation."

It brought me back to my childhood,
when my family owned a set of binoculars.

Once, as a grade school student,
the teenager next door warned everybody
in the neighborhood ahead of time that
he was having a party in the backyard,
so they should come to him if the noise got to
be too loud. So I climbed up the top
of the tree in my front yard with the

binoculars to spy on the party. Things
were going fine till someone saw me spying,
and said, "Hi, Pee-Wee."

A few years later, as a pre-adolescent,
my next door neighbor's wife was out in
her yard sunbathing right in front of my window,
and I had a good view. So I went to get the
binoculars, and I was alarmed to see her
husband sitting where she was lying down,
laughing and waving in the direction of
the window. Another time, I spied on the
same couple in the tree with the binoculars,
looking into their window, and I saw the
husband bite the wife on her rear end. I
heard her scream through the window.
I must've been thoroughly jealous.

In this day and age, anybody could be
spying on anybody. There are cameras everywhere,
and binoculars are ancient technology. But I
guess they could have a purpose. I could always
go bird watching, but the animal rights activists
would say, "By going out and watching birds,
you're disrupting them in their natural
habitat," or some such thing. I guess being
"observant" and "nosy" are two different
extremes. But I'm forty-five now, and I'm
no longer nosy, because things in old age
cease to be exciting really quickly. Like
this prose poem. Sorry, dear reader, if

your attention span at this point is finding you getting bored. I'm done. You may be excused.

GETTING TO THE TRUTH

by

LYNN HOFFMAN

do you ever dismember
the dreams you screamed
when you were a kid?
you didn't really lose those dreams,
they hung around like parrots on your shoulder,
like gnats in august that live 'til christmas,
and they whisper to you.

the secret to putting yourself back together
(when you're broken)
is to let the dreams be trumpets,
little tootin' tutelaries.

sometimes you get stuck in a drunk,
trapped in the liquor loop.

you'd repeat yourself if
there was any self left to repeat.
you know the feeling, don't you?
and you know what's going on?
you're in one of those dreams,
the one about building the boat
but the lake is made out of little white stones
or the one where you and your friends
are all inside a bubble barrel
and you're trying to build a school
in the middle of the swimming pool
and there's this one girl who isn't
(really) pretty but she knows something
about you or maybe about swimming pools
or was it skimming tools?
and she has a lisp and … she's sordid beautiful.
you know that feeling, don't you?

just wondrin'.

HUSH, HUSH

by
LEN KUNTZ

She's had enemies before but never this. This one smells like warm bread mixed with honeysuckle and lime, its eyes too big, its neck nearly nonexistent.

She thinks that maybe her mind is subverting her. After all, her own mother was crazy as a loon and even became institutionalized. Everyone knows insanity is hereditary.

Still, it's as if there are dozens of knives pinched at the back of her neck, threatening malice or death if she doesn't go ahead, go forward.

It doesn't help that no one understands, not her husband or best friend or brother. They don't say so, but she knows they think she's evil, unstable, the worst human ever.

Though she's thought about it, she would never hurt the infant. *Would she?*

No, she's not as horrid as the others think. *Is she?*

The baby gurgles and coos and flaps its chubby doll arms and doll legs. If she was as happy and lazy and as taken care of as a baby she'd be cheerful, too. And maybe that's the problem—she's jealous of her own child, resentful of her husband who's never home and has no idea about colic or jaundice or having nipples shredded from breastfeeding.

She can't remember now if she'd ever wanted this baby in the first place. It was someone's idea. Had to be. She and Matthew were planners, tacticians. Now, as a couple, they are sulfur, gunpowder, a heap of ash.

There it goes again, squalling, its face a rictus, a doll monster come to life.

She's sung a thousand nursery rhymes, rocked the thing back and forth in her lap a thousand times, and yet the endless circle still swirls.

The wailing goes on and on. She tells herself *This is it. No more. I can't do it.*

* * *

When her husband comes home two days later he seems interested for once and the first thing he asks is about the infant. "Where's Rose?"

"Upstairs sleeping."

She follows her husband up the steps, following close behind, wondering if she should tell him first, confess.

When he opens the door to the nursery Rose coos as if it knows Dad's home.

"Aren't you just so precious," her husband says, leaning down into the crib.

She feels those knives again, pressed against the back of her neck. It's her imagination, but she feels something warm and liquid leak down her shoulders. She cranes her head so that the blades catch more skin and steps backwards, testing both the strength of her fear and resolve.

When the baby starts to wail, she moves to the crib, brushing past her husband, taking the baby in her arms, saying to her husband, "Go change. Relax. You've had a long day," and to the whining baby she whispers, "Hush, hush. Let me tell you something, something true. You're going to get through this. Yes you will. Be strong."

THE TRUE DEFENSE OF BILL B.

by

DANIELLE DAVIS

I was a better man, before.
Not locked in a cage, impatient,
waiting for my next great adventure.
I chose my words carefully
when I called it an accident
since the lawyers read into things.
Speaking for the dead,
with my rose-splattered hands
making Rorschach tests dried brown on the walls.
The prosecutors called it
A lie.
I didn't kill those girls.
When I said I didn't do it,

the jury didn't believe me–
it's hard to spin a story from the truth.
The only guilty man in prison–
everyone on the inside claims innocence but I'm
the only one telling the truth.
Out of the whole group, the lawyer's
right: innocent men get left behind.
I'm left to rot though I tried to get it
right. Down to the last memory,
their hair haunts my dreams:
sticky crimson rope
streaked with skin like lamb's ears,
the strands wouldn't come off my hands...
the night they lost their innocence.
I revel in the memories from before,
When I was a free man, patient,
Enjoying the wind down the highway,
The throttle in my ears,
the bars, (the girls in the bars).
Some things you can't get back once they're lost.
I regret that more than anything.

(now read backwards for *The Admission of Bill B.*)

SO, ABOUT THAT ENGAGEMENT

by

M. EARL SMITH

So, you meet someone online, and you have little idea how much, if any, importance they'll have in your life. It's hard to gauge, ya know? But sometimes, you hit a perfect storm, and she's brilliant and boisterous and beautiful and whatever other adjective that starts with the letter B that you can think of.

I had no intentions, however, of breaking her engagement. And that's the truth...more or less.

I met 'Connie' in a writer's forum. She was 30, the same age as I, and, ironically, headed back to college, just as I was. She was headed to a prestigious institution in the American Northeast, and I was pondering my options after community college. After some late night discussions, she insisted that I apply to one of the prestigious Ivy League schools on the East Coast.

I thought she was out of her damned mind, but she was right. I got in. And thus started an online friendship that would blossom, at least for me, into feelings so deep that I couldn't help but to wonder if I ever felt anything for my ex-wife.

There was only one problem: Connie was engaged.

To her credit, (and mine), we were determined to do things the right way. How we felt was established early on, and, although she did an amazing job at keeping me at arm's length, there was no shortage of romantic gestures on my part. Sure, I convinced myself that it was, in truth, just a series of writing exercises, but there was little doubt in the desire of my heart.

We talked about it, and the 'what-ifs' were all slanted in my favor, but her loyalty was resolute. In retrospect, that was one of the things that drove me to her. Who wouldn't want someone that loyal in the face of such a temptation? It's not so much that I saw myself as that tempting; however, sometimes, the pieces fit together so painfully well that you can't help but to writhe in pain...and in pleasure.

Back in May, Connie sent me a text while I was visiting family in Ohio: her engagement was over. And while a part of me rejoiced, another part of me was sad. She was bound and determined to see things to fruition with 'Corey' and yet there had to be a small part of her agonizing for the same that I agonized for. To see someone I cared for so much fail, hurt me, even if such a failure would sate my own selfish desires.

We're not dating yet, but I think we're close. There's long weekends in New England, where things are kept platonic, at least physically, although the conversation veers to children, to a life beyond what we have now.

I'll keep reaching. And, truth be told, I hope she does too.

LEARNING FROM THE HEART

by

WAYNE SCHEER

I didn't feel much splayed out in my hospital bed the morning of my heart surgery. I had already been given, I discovered later, an amnesiac, so I have no memory of being wheeled to the operating room, my family following alongside. I guess that moment is reserved for made-for-television movies.

What I do remember is the night before in the hospital room, just after the nurse injected "something to help you sleep," into one of the many tubes attached from my arm to a machine in back of my bed. I could hear my wife trying to swallow her sobs and my daughter-in-law sniffling while my son tried consoling them. The nurse said they would have to leave and, as my wife and daughter-in-law kissed my cheek and forehead, I heard my son whisper in my ear, "Dad, if you die it would really piss me off."

I tried joking about how it would ruin my plans for the weekend as well.

In all honesty, survival hadn't been a major fear going into the operation, although I was apprised of the risks. Whether it was my ability to suppress, a blind trust in a surgeon I had only recently met, or the simple resignation that comes from having no better options, death remained an abstract concept.

After all, if I died, chances were good I wouldn't know it.

They say there are no atheists in foxholes, but I found the opposite to be true. I took solace in my suspicion that there was no afterlife, no God waiting to judge me. I wouldn't spend eternity learning lessons I failed to achieve in this world. My sins and virtues would be as irrelevant as last week's newspaper. Consciousness would simply end.

It was after the operation that I began feeling anxiety as I observed the worry on my wife's face and the half-closed eyes of my son and daughter-in-law who had been dividing time between their children and the hospital. This sounds rather shallow, I know. Of course, I understood how much my wife loved me and how devastated she would be had I died. Of course, I understood the same was true for my son and his family, especially the grandchildren who liked to climb on me pretending I was a ladder. But there is nothing like lying in a hospital bed, in a morphine-induced stupor, tubes sticking out of your arms, neck and stomach, to help you realize how important your insignificant place in the universe really is. And how much your family means to you.

I matter. My life matters. It's the kind of insight that sounds almost silly saying it aloud. But, like my son's joke, it offered me inspiration to focus on my recovery. It seems surprisingly clear: it's who I love and who loves me here and now that matters.

I find that truth reassuring.

IN THE TWINKLING OF AN EYE

by

SALLY RENO

I thought I saw a water nixie just as the sun was rising above Haggs Hill. I saw the flash of her tail as she leaped to greet the sun. Arms upraised, her vanilla skin and silvery hair reached to grab the light. It was in the little hollow where Upper Superstition Creek squeezes through the rock wall to spill into a deep pool. The abrupt height of the summits all around keeps the hollow and its pool in deep shadow both early and late but I had come through the gap at the moment of glory.

She must have believed she was alone, so I watched awhile in stillness as her wild leaping, twisting and splashing sent a thousand sparkles skittering across the water. Then, not wishing to intrude upon her rites, I slipped away. It was only at the end of day, as I ate my supper by lantern light and heard that the little Greenleigh girl had gone missing, that I knew the truth of what I had witnessed.

THE STRANGE CASE OF THE DEAD FAERIES

by

VIVIAN WAGNER

She said she found a dead faerie. None of us in the faerie workshop were inclined to question her. We'd paid ten dollars, after all, to hear something just like this. The faerie had blonde hair and translucent, glittery skin and wore a green dress, as, apparently, the northern Ohio species is wont to do.

Our teacher told us she picked the faerie up, carefully, and buried it in the garden. The dogs watched.

The next day, a neighbor called and told our teacher about some weird, colorful insect, dead on the deck.

"It looks almost human!" cried the neighbor, distraught.

Our faerie workshop teacher walked over to her neighbor's house, and sure enough, it turned out to be another faerie.

"Someone must have been spraying chemicals," our teacher told us. "Sad, but it makes total sense."

The neighbor refused to believe it was a faerie, insisting it was an insect. But the thing is, said our teacher, she must not have looked closely enough at its tiny, pale face.

PENNY FOR YOUR THOUGHTS

by

PAUL BECKMAN

"Sweet," Mirsky said looking at the mother / daughter pass in front of him while he sat people watching on a bench in the mall.

"Which one?" asked the forty-something year old sitting on the other end of the bench.

"Uh oh," Mirsky thought. "I said that out loud." He folded his newspaper that he was pretending to read and looked over at her.

"Her" was an attractive brunette not even pretending to obscure her people watching with any of the usual reading materials that people use as a ruse.

She stared at Mirsky long enough to make him uncomfortable. "Pardon me," he said.

"You said 'sweet' and I just wondered if you were thinking of the mother or the daughter. That's all."

"You see," Mirsky said. "Truth be told, I have a mental condition which causes me, on occasion, to say aloud what I think I'm only thinking to myself."

"I see," she said and turned away as Mirsky re-opened his newspaper.

"You wonder if I'll have lunch with you," she said tossing him an attractive smile. "Were you asking me or thinking to yourself of asking me? That's quite a gimmick you've got going there—kind of like a mental Tourette's that you can hide behind."

Mirsky knew that he neither thought nor asked her aloud about lunch but for a split-second he had a doubt.

"Emily," she said getting up from the bench. "And yes, sushi would be fine, thank you."

Mirsky stood up, dropped his paper on the bench, took Emily's hand and walked off into the unknown.

HONESTLY

by
MICHAEL KONIK

Folks who begin sentences about themselves with the word "honestly" are subtly implying that there are times, perhaps many times – this particular time when they're talking to you being an exception, of course – when they're not really honest. That's why they're prefacing their personal revelation with a qualifier, a certification of authenticity. This time, you can be assured, they're not being dishonest, and it's good to be reminded.

Honestly, I didn't think I could ever write an essay this open and vulnerable.

This must be a mistake, I thought. These "honestly" people probably mean to say "candidly." They're making what used to be known in the days of Strunk & White as a "usage error." Since I'm accustomed to hearing passing pedestrians (most of them under-30) use the word "like" dozens of times – honestly, dozens! – during a single burst of oratory, the degradation of our collective language skills no longer surprises. Multi-syllabic words and the dictionary-using elite intellectuals who utter them are no longer respected; they're mocked.

But then I was inside a corporate calorie store buying some corporate calories, feeling, like, you know, sort of like not very good about, like, supporting? Like, the whole system thing? Honestly, I was a little bummed. But whatevers. Corporately produced music was playing loudly from hidden speakers. A boy singer was wailing about love, as singers tend to. I'm not sure what the song was called, but the first word of each line was – and, you guys, I am so not kidding – it was "honestly."

> *Honestly [insert confession here]*
> *Honestly [insert description of feelings here]*
> *Honestly [etcetera]*

I'm starting to understand that the popular culture, including the way people talk, reflects our popular conception of truth: that it's not an absolute; rather, it has various versions, some of which involve candor and some of which involve honesty, and all of which may be selected as the appropriate truth for whatever fits the circumstances.

The Japanese language uses the words *honne* and *tatemae* to describe the contrast between a person's private thoughts, feelings and desires (*honne*) and the behavior and opinions displayed publicly (*tatemae,* which translates literally to "façade"). *Honne,* the authentic truth, is often contrary to societal expectations or class assumptions. One's honest reality is meant to be hidden, except, perhaps, with one's closest intimates. *Tatemae* is the opposite: It's what's expected by society, and it need not match the *honne*.

If you wish to avoid conflict, be quasi-"popular," and encourage others to never know the real you, the *tatemae* path works charmingly.

If you wish to be someone who almost never prefaces her sentences with "honestly," someone whose entire life isn't built on fraudulent perception but on transparent realness, the *honne* path will take you there and beyond, as it leads, ultimately, to enlightenment.

The truth is out there, and inside all of us. Behaving *honestly* is the first step to knowing it.

90% OF ALL SOURDOUGH TURTLES

BREAK APART IN THE WATER ON THEIR VERY FIRST TRIP TO THE SEA

by

DAVID S. ATKINSON

Garth Algar really ruins a trip to the Ripley's Believe It or Not! museum. You remember...the sidekick guy from *Wayne's World*? He kept following me around as I looked at exhibits, trying to decide whether I believed or not, and loudly asserting the latter.

And it was supposed to be the highlight of my annual National Pickle Week vacation to the San Francisco waterfront.

The honest congressman from Borneo? "Not!" The tomato a Michigan househusband grew as big as a pumpkin that also looked exactly like a pumpkin and was made out of pumpkin? "Not!" The volleyball-sized sweat ruby bearing a mysterious curse causing whomever came into possession of it to pay a substantial and expensive luxury tax? "Not!"

It was pretty annoying, honestly. I can see why the guy hadn't worked since the films, that and only being a character instead of an actual person. Museum staff kept suggesting I leave so he'd go too, but they stopped short of actually deigning to speak to him about the problem.

His kind of negativity spoils the whole intent of that sort of museum. People go there for curiosity, sure. However, it's the ambiguous state that's the real draw. Like Denny's. The exhibits are so fantastic...you can't quite believe...but it's all true. Well, true more or less. They've stretched a few things...such as Nixon's high score on Pac-Man. Agnew might have played a couple levels while Tricky was in the bathroom. Still, you get the idea. You get how Garth's skepticism killed the mood.

So...you understand what I had to do.

And that's the truth. I realize you asked me why I was carving Steve McQueen's face into the back of the Statue of Liberty's head, but I stand by what I've said...more or less.

THE SIGN ON THE BAR

by

A J HUFFMAN

said Jesus loves beer too,
and I almost pissed
myself laughing at the plausible
truth of that statement
and the blasphemous sarcasm
I was sure it intended.
I could not help but wonder
what inspired this moment
of literary genius: an angry discourse
with a reborn bible thumper just out
of AA, maybe an angry mob of spinsters
denied donation for their latest fund-
raising project, or it might have been just
a long-haired client running his hand
along a water glass's rim, trying to decide

if he should will it into something stronger.
In any event, I made a note to stop
in on my return trip, thank the owner for not
only continuing the much appreciated work
of tastefully preventing dehydration, but also
for the rare miracle of bringing a
much-needed spot

of laughter to an otherwise overwhelmingly
hopeless day.

BUT THIS ONE IS TRUE

by

JACK GRANATH

Today, like any other day,
began with my plain need for sleep
ceding to obdurate desire
through several stages of confusion.
I didn't know the woman, though
I thought by thinking hard enough
I would. The feeling didn't leave me.
God knows what finally got me up,
compunction, shower, cup of mud.
Whatever it was was not enough
to shake that apparition off.
All day I found me in my mind
padding along behind her, trying,
with lots of help from the absurd,
to win her love. At last, I bolted,

cruised my blighted city streets
on foot for hours, and wound up in
the neighborhood of nightfall
milling through the shadowed shelves,
concave beneath a weight of books,
in some small, plainly failing shop.
Today, like any other day:
except for the epiphany
that came on with a terrifying
lack of dramatic crux or closure.
I know it isn't possible,
but there she marvelously was,
exactly as I pictured her,
the big, sad eyes, the sulky mouth,
bare shoulders tilting expertly
beneath a wilderness of hair,
continuous distraction for
the sturdy man that she was with.
The sturdy man that she was with—
how fatuously unexpected.
That nagging feeling I had had
all day, I understood it then.
She was the sort of dream girl who
wouldn't have anything to do
with those lost souls that do the dreaming.
And, lo, she didn't. Disappointment
would be busy for a while,
I knew, attending to its wounds,
building a nest inside the giant terror

that such unlikeliness inspired.
So I went home to get some sleep,
to burrow in and rest my feet
and start the whole damn thing again.

IF IT CHEEKILY BIT

by

TIM PHILIPPART

Would one know truth, if
truth bit one on the butt?
There are times when I long
for the mirror to reveal,
as I awkwardly turn,
some teeth marks on my right cheek.
Truth didn't always seem ethereal.
It used to set you free.
Look at the politicians, the diplomats.
the negotiators, poker players, con men,
and women.

Truth is as welcome as Sarin.

MY RELIGION

by
MARTIN JON PORTER

"And I shall be there when the earth and the air
Are rent from sea to sky"
~ extract from untitled poem, Jack London

As a boy,
I learned that the ceiling
would always be white

bread the body of Christ
red wine the blood of Christ
and water protection of the Holy Spirit.

As a man,
through cracks in this same ceiling
I can now see –
blue, yellow, orange, pink, red, grey, black
and sometimes white

bread gives my body energy,
red wine is a similar colour to blood
and water is only holy to developing countries.

Thanks be to Life.

IN PRISM

by

MARTIN SHAW

In my life, machines amassed by forklift, dressed in pig iron skirts of racing green, precision welded for keener corners. Oil pooled, like hot butter reflecting yellow sodium bulbs, while metal elbows pumped fists that churned rotunda bellies, moulding fridge doors and cheap tin trays for the Christmas countdown...

With paper underarm, a machine minder, Buddy Blue, sits down on his plastic chair facing the lights and dials. He's on a ten-till-six-shift, his face as pallid as the paper readouts from the computer at his side.

Deep into the night, Buddy's head drops to his chest. The workshop manager notices. He looks stern as he strides over to wake him, then quickly calls the stretcher bearers, the appointed first aiders, upon seeing Buddy's lips as dark as his last name. They try to resuscitate him on the spot, before finding a whiz-bang defibrillator for a jump start. But with blood already coagulated after years of working on tectonic concrete floors, Buddy's body has already been zombified with thrombosis – he's as dead as the proverbial door nail.

Buddy's unmanned machine flashes inter-mittent red lights in sympathy, and even the computer readout is jammed, the paper concertinaed, like an accordion out of air and tune. The whole factory is shut down for ten minutes, and the graphs in the office fall from the top of an ink drawn Mount Everest, onto the true marker dots below.

All of us workers hear a radio playing from above, then realise it hasn't been switched off for years. A game of musical chairs begins. The guy who replaces me, set free from his incarceration of stores, is shackled again by compulsory overtime. After a pay rise, it's myself who replaces Buddy Blue – I watch his work life pass in the flash of neon lights before me, while mine is being re-mapped on the computer, climbing to the top k2.

MY MOTHER: THE LIAR

by

SYLVIA AGUILAR-ZÉLENY

I am thirtysomething years old, I am with a group of friends eating Chinese food. I say "Mhh, I simply love bamboo!" Someone says, "Bamboo? That's not bamboo, those are water chestnuts." He puts one in his mouth. "No, it's bamboo, my mother told me it was bamboo." After a long argument with my friends about bamboo and water chestnuts, I realize this was probably one of my mother's lies. I see her saying: "Yes, baby, it's bamboo. Pandas eat bamboo, come on, try them." I see myself as a little girl, giving them a try, eating and then loving them, because pandas loved them.

But, that wasn't bamboo. My mother had lied.

My mother lied about the silliest things in the world. She lied about her age, which I guess is normal for anyone who refuses to grow old, but she also lied about her zodiac sign. Who does that? When asked, she would always say: "I am Gemini. Just like my brother." Now that I write about it, I see how this lie says more about her than anything else. She said she was Gemini as a way to prove her strong relationship with her brother, who raised her when they were both orphaned. He was the reason she "became" Gemini.

Have I mentioned that she also lied about her blood type?

It happened in August of 2014. She had been in the hospital for weeks, she needed blood and the hospital did not have it. All of us, my brother, my father looked for people to donate A+ blood for our sick mother. The first person who came to donate blood was rejected. At the lab the conversation went like this:

"We need AB-, your friend is A+."

"Why do you need AB-? She is A+?"

"No, your mother is AB-."

"No way."

"Your mother is AB-."

"No, she isn't, she's always said she is A+."

The guy showed us a paper that stated the truth. My mother was AB-, period. Seriously, who lies about their blood type?

Eventually we did get the blood my mother needed, but neither the blood nor the doctors could do anything else. Cancer had already taken her small bruised body. She and the truth about many other things died on September 6th, 2014.

There's a song from an artist my mom liked (or so she said). The song is titled 'Él Me Mintió', it's about a woman complaining of the lies of her lover. There's a line that says: "Mentira todo era mentira / palabras al viento / tan solo un capricho que el niño tenía." Which translates to: "Lie everything was a lie / words to the wind / just the whim of a child." I wonder if my mother's lies were more of a whim, the whims of the child she never got to be because life forced her to grow up too soon. Perhaps she was not a liar, just a bit whimsical.

WHEELCHAIR

by
RUTH Z. DEMING

You've seen them in the
supermarkets, the elderly
men and women, riding
in motorized wheelchairs,
"as a courtesy to our valued
customers." My left foot is
encased in an orthopedic
boot, the little toe broken
and weeping silently inside.

My daughter Sarah has come
to live with me and use my
home as a Writers Retreat.
"You can do it, Mom," she
says as I climb into the
wheelchair, unplug the fat
black plug from the wall
and cruise slowly into

the wall-to-wall traffic
of the Giant Supermarket.

Grasp the yellow handles
this is where the power
comes from. Why, it's
like driving a car or riding
a bike.

"You're doing great Mom,"
says Sarah as we glide
like a horse, me, and the jockey,
her, down the long produce aisle
for watermelon, broccoli, black
kale, zucchini and yellow squash
and all the other things she will
cook for me on her retreat.

Never a mistake I make, as I
navigate around the huge barricades
– o do not crash – of featured
products, potato chips of all
different hues – new beers they
now stock – and – what's this?
snow shovels already, though
it's still the dog days
of August.

At seventy years old, I am
proud of myself. I have
learned something new. No
cryptograms or crosswords
or learning Japanese for me.

Just the simple act of driving
in a car through the Giant
Supermarket on a hot August
day with my beloved daughter
and kidney donor by my side.

AMERICAN DREAM: THE MOVIE

by

JOHN LAMBREMONT, SR.

The premise of the film
is somewhat unusual, in that
the same recurring dream script
is performed and recorded three times;
with each version shot separately,
but all three are intended
to be identical in all particulars.

The object lesson is that despite
the most meticulous attention to detail,
none of the repeated episodes
looks or feels exactly the same;
no fly can stay on the same wall forever,
shadows inevitably grow longer,
and voices reciting the same lines
contain subtle changes in nuance
that are easily and readily discerned.

By the end of the third repetition,
the viewer realizes that he or she
is the dreamer.

THAT MAN IN HER LIFE

by

JOHN GREY

She never did lie
but the truth didn't know that.
How could it be otherwise?
Her face was blessed with eternal light
as she moved from neon to neon,
danced like wind,
cried out like ocean birds.
Her honesty was blue as in eyes,
or painted like her cheeks.
It was slim and dainty enough to handle touch.
And, best of all, it could slip backward
in high heels,
measure stripped of rhythm,
a fine thread connecting
leftover laughter to love.

And lies could only struggle to keep up,
to imitate badly in the recklessness
of other women.
Truth held her head up,
the one and only person in her flesh,
proud and seductive and indelible.
I took the truth's hand.
I swirled around,
too dizzy to believe.
Light be damned,
I convinced myself
life is nothing but shade.
A hair fell from a golden thatch.
A tear followed.
She grew older.
She was deceived at last.
Such is the truth
when the lies have at it.

FREE RANGE

by
EM KÖNIG

I watched then
Laced my hands with clean soil.
I want to bury this stuff
If the ground will forgive me.

I shook off the images
And wrote down the words:
Ten thousand birds.

The Minister signed it off,
It is her call after all
To decide how much space
A lady needs to move.

I shook off the images
And wrote down the words
Meaningful and regular.
But what is meaningful?
And what is regular?

REDEMPTION SONG

by

BRIAN OBIRI-ASARE

They were under an open sky, in a scrubby little park where everything was shifting except the clouds, and beneath these clouds, seated in a field of force of conversation and silence, it seemed as if the world contained only them – fragile, human bodies.

There was a little taper of a fire going, nothing much, and amid these men – hobos and drifters – there was a junkie kid who reminded Pete of himself from way back, the same combination of despair and hope holding out against all odds. A junkie yarning with the others as if it didn't matter: a sense had already formed that at some point soon he'd be cast off, left to fight for himself.

Two bottles of Jim Bean and one of a nameless cough mixture were doing the rounds. And for a while not much was said besides the occasional shit, fuck, a revelation from the past in the form of a grunt, until eventually – because it had to at some point – banter started between the man named Bullman and the man named Doctor Love, the kind of trash talk that comes after a long quiet. Then the man called Bullman told a story about a car crash.

Two cars, allegedly doing one forty on a stretch of highway outside Darwin, struck each other head-on, and from the wreckage a one year old emerged unscathed. This led to an argument about the possibility of such an event, which in turn led to a story about a guy who lost his arm in a farming accident, which in turn morphed into chit chat about time on the inside, which in turn led to stories about knives, stories about the best way to stab another man if the need arose.

At that point, the junkie kid came in off topic, telling a wild tale about an old Warlpiri man who claimed his baby daughter had been spirited away by a wedge-tailed eagle, which led to a brief argument about the possibility of such an event, which somehow led back to knives and then silence.

And in this stretch of silence Pete held his own knife story close to his chest and resisted the urge to join in, because to tell it truthfully he'd have to explain how he'd spent a couple of years with an old meth addict named Wishbone and there was no way he'd ever speak to anyone about the deep extent of their sharing. He'd never tell anyone about Wishbone's eyes in the end, all wet and pleading. He'd never tell anyone what he realised in that moment – a man seeing far beyond the clouds, far beyond his housing commission flat, far beyond time and his place in the world.

So instead of words, out of Pete's lips came a melody so fragile it almost vanished into thin air. A melody that broke through the field of force of conversation and silence and heat and provided a balm to spread over the gathered brokenness.

THINKING BETTER OF IT

by

PATRICIA WALSH

Travel on satellite and a prayer.
Minding one's own business, beyond censure
Eating kale crisps to sate conscience
Coming over strange is not your fault.

Fainting in the tattooist's chair
Leaving it up to the hairdresser
The same argument resting on another's case
A day out would help matters, no real type.

An open window cauterises sleep
Illusions and delusions step in to help.
Jesus dying for the ungodly, a happy disposition
Calling back salvation where it lies.

Start local. The dead don't need the money.
Hurting through the pocket a lesson supreme
God should have given us a written exam
To see what's regurgitated in order to pass.

Pigeons in unison, fly to rooftops
In perfect time, eating the scraps
No one cared to muster, not even the binmen
Serving a purpose otherwise denied.

We all have a purpose, like it or not,
A calling despite ourselves, from our comfy
            situation
Casting a cold eye over future accomplishments
Being good for its own sake is best.

A MOST PROMISING BOYFRIEND'S DAUGHTER'S PERSPECTIVE

by

SAMUEL COLE

He's not mother's replacement. Nor a step-father.
Nor commonplace among friends. Or family.
Society is friendlier, for sure. But still. Not
everybody approves. Or gets it. Mom

remains quiet, throwing snark-bombs in
the annual Christmas letter—the best place
for *gay* to come out and own its truth

among the sassy spirits of the season.
Where (and when) did Dad meet him?
They speak gym, Trivago, NFL, Herberger's.
They hold hands in the car, on the street,

at the store, during movies. If Dad held Mom's
hand, I don't remember or understand man-crush
softness—*hey there cutie-sweets*—which pains
me for Mom, who isn't dating, nor is she soft,

marinating poorly in Dad's fiery, rejection stew.
Perhaps this is why she does not hug me.
Nor my brother. One-sided questions of intimacy
she cannot toss aside or hold too close. I get it.

Detach from any genetic reminder of who
he is. Or was. I do not blame her. Nor do I pry.
My dad is honest so I believe he did not trick her.
He is kind so I believe he did not mistreat her.

He is solid so I believe he did not intend to
leave her hollow, moving around the house as if
everything within it is a misplaced nickname.
My dad is happy so I believe he does not regret

taking the risk of moving on. And out. My brother
agrees, adds eye-rolls, wrist-flicks, &
  stereotype-slurs.
My dad is anti-typecast, quite unlike his...spouse?
Friends ask if I (she, we) feel betrayed, lied to,

bamboozled, eclipsed. I do not. And why should I?
Like Dad, and Mom, I also enjoy watching
  a novelty
act reach the zenith of its dwindling
  attractiveness.

A REGULAR MAN

by

DANNY P. BARBARE

As if this is who I am

a fork and a knife

I'm a regular man

who works a menial

　job

neither poor nor rich

who tries to drink

a cold one when I can.

AUTHOR-IZED ALTERATIONS

by

CARL 'PAPA' PALMER

not actually how it may have happened
but maybe how I wish it would have
occurred or could come about if ever
that circumstance should emerge again

as an author I am able to alter any event
change outcomes actions and answers
make it different and do it all over again
when or wherever by use of written words

perhaps hoping you'll read what I wrote
believe that it really did happen that way
possibly change more than just the story
maybe change how I get along with you

CONTEMPORARY CENSORSHIP

by
MICHAEL MARROTTI

I've been banned
from the Brookline
open Mic for reciting
poetry that makes
pseudo-liberals
feel uncomfortable

Excluded from
the feminist
lit magazines
over the make
of my reproductive
organ

Too white for
the all black
poetry submission
somehow that's
copacetic
nobody is
complaining

One closed door
after another
target on my head
for being born
into this race
and gender
forced to endure
unapologetic
censorship

No tears to be shed
no wars to be lost
I've been singled out
most of my life
this is exactly
what I'm after

The beginning
equates to this

The end

MA'AM? CAN YOU TELL ME YOUR NAME?

by

BARBARA RUTH

"Good morning." A young man with black wavy hair and a white coat enters the room. "I'm Dr. Abel. Do you know where you are?"

Where should I begin? Do I think it's a good morning? What exactly is this doctor able to do? And what does he mean by 'where am I' anyway?

He takes out a stethoscope, aims it at my belly. Does he expect to hear what I say while he's listening to my abdomen, or does he think I might speak from my belly button? He looks up at me inquiringly, removes the stethoscope, presses across my abdomen, up into my stomach. It hurts but I say nothing. He still looks at me with question marks; I know I'm supposed to speak. "I'm in a

73

hospital bed."

"Do you know what hospital this is?"

"Stanford?" I remember Stanford, I even remember coming in through the Emergency Room, some time, maybe last month. I remember an ER yesterday.

"Ma'am, take off your headphones, maybe you'll be able to hear me better."

I wish Wavy Hair would at least tell me if I answered the question correctly.

"I can hear you with them on. They're Bose noise canceling headphones, but the truth is they're only noise reducing. They cut out some of the sounds on my epilepsy channels, that's why I need them. There are so many noises here that could give me a seizure. I'd really like to leave them on." He looms closer, the waves of his hair make me seasick so I look down. Shiny black shoes, the leather cracking across the top of the foot. How can that be comfortable? Why did some cow have to die for these ugly, uncomfortable shoes?

"Can you tell me what city we're in?"

I wish he'd tell me if I got the hospital question right. "Palo Alto?" Again, nothing from Dr. Wavy Hair Abel. He'd make a terrible teacher, but a good test proctor.

"Ma'am? Can you tell me your name?"

"How much time have you got?"

"I have other patients to see. Just tell me your name."

Sometimes I'm pretty good at handling doctors,

but not this doctor, not today, "Patricia Isabella. Some people call me PI. My father called me $\prod$. You know, like in math? Then there are some personal names – well, everybody has those, right? You probably have some yourself. Pet names, used in the family or by a person's sweetheart. My brother calls me Pat, and my mother calls me Patty. So you see why it takes a while to answer the question." I should stop there. I should have stopped before there. I can't find the brakes. "Do you want to hear some of the things PI can stand for? It's way beyond Private Investigator and Politically Incorrect. There's Potential Instability, Probability Index, Post-Ictal, People's Initiative – that's one of my favorites. Public Intoxication, that's not one of my favorites. Practically Insolvent, that's the harsh reality."

THE LIZARD QUEEN

by

STEPHEN V. RAMEY

Dave says it. "You look more than happy, man, you look ex-static." As he speaks, he twists the rope, twists the rope tighter. Sylvester's smile twists into a grimace.

"Spill the beans," Dave says, pushing his face close to Sylvester's steamed-shit mouth. Broken teeth, rotted gums, tongue gone to leather and back. "Spill it, man. Tell me where she is. You're not that sexy anymore."

Sylvester spits, but all he musters is a foam that floats away. *Bubble bath Brahms*, he thinks, and somehow he chuckles despite the pain.

"What the fuck!" Dave yells. "What do I got to do to get through? What are you laughing about now?"

Sylvester's lips move, a sigh. "Syl vee ah... ahh...

ahhhhh," and he's chuckling again, the noise muffled in the soundproofed room. Sylvia used to compliment his laughter; they'd lie in bed after *it* and he'd laugh as she flicked, flicked, the cigarette trembling in the grip of her sweet lips. Sylvia and Sylvester. Worth another laugh.

"That's right, man. Sylvia. Where is she laying low?" Dave releases the rope and relief floods Sylvester. His shoulders hunch forward until his torso hangs from the harness. He tries to kneel. The rope does not provide that much slack.

Dave paces. The room is narrow and long. Sylvester watches through half-lidded eyes as light smears and splashes, now an infinite ocean in this finite space. There is no escape; it will only continue until Dave has extracted what he craves.

Sylvester's head falls limp from his corded neck. Blood drools onto floor tile. The pattern reminds him of the tired red tattoo on Sylvia's hip. *Life is balance between holding on and letting go.* She told him that, and now, at last, he believes it's true.

SIDE-BY-SIDE

by

RUTH SABATH ROSENTHAL

my sister and I, a truly chubby pair
of identical-twin toddles riding for hours
two matching cylinder-shaped
green leather hassocks daily. Snacking
along the way, occasionally falling off,
we suffered injuries our busy parents couldn't see:
The hurt of shut-ins riding as far as
their little wanting minds could, stuck in one
another's company nonstop — me taking the lead,
always, my sister always trying to catch up.

And just feet from our play space, a green cut-
velvet sofa with a painting hanging above
that regularly had us climbing onto
the ample cushions, where we'd stand,
side-by-side, gazing up at a young woman

in a long see-through dress and a young man
clad only in a cloth wrapped waist-to-thigh.
Man and woman running side-by-side from
something while holding, over their heads,
what looked to be an unraveled length of what he
      was wearing.

Now, nearly a half century later, with the
passing of my twin (she, who having lived
alone
her entire adult life, said she hated her life,
didn't have a life and never would!), I've found
myself thinking about the two green leather
      hassocks,
the green cut-velvet sofa and the mesmerizing
painting
that we, a pair of truly chubby twin tots, stood
side-by-side gazing upon, in what felt like
a forever life to me.

FIRST LOVE

by

IRENE BUCKLER

They have been together for fifteen years and he still remembers the thrill of seeing her for the first time. He knew instantly that he had to have her, no matter what. She had the looks. She had the class and her body was perfect, but only later when they were alone together, did he realise that it was the way that she responded, almost intuitively, to his touch that set her apart from all others. No matter where he wanted to go or when, she was always ready, too – and they went places he had never been before. She has never let him down.

He sighs. Raking through these memories only makes his decision harder, but it has to be made. Things have changed. His needs have changed and it is time to move on.

He lingers over the photos he has just taken of her. He is not as trim as he used to be, but she has not changed a bit. She is still gorgeous.

With some reluctance, he fills out her details, nominates the price he wants and uploads the photos on the car sales site. Now that he is married and has a child on the way, he needs a family car, but he will never forget his first true love.

BOOKS CANNOT SAVE US

by

ROBBI NESTER

In the very center of the living room,
my father sat, a sentinel,
and watched the news.
Even if he fell asleep, I didn't dare
turn the channel or switch off the set.
I never knew when he'd explode,
and off would come the belt.

Like any prey, I knew enough to flee.
I'd run downstairs, wet laundry
on the indoor clothesline
slapping at my arms,
to reach the door.
Even once I turned the balky lock,
I had nowhere to go.

Should I head down Stirling
to the playground,
or up the avenue, my father
roaring in my wake?

No one would help.
The neighbors only sneered.
I knew I'd pay the price—
for what, I wasn't sure,
would have to bear the belt,
and worse, his screaming face,
veins bulging like an ivy vine
squeezing a tree to death.

Once he caught me,
as he always did, I'd
cast about for strategies.
Once I threw myself
across the room,
by the aquarium,
where the bookshelf stood,
filled with *Aesop's Fables,*
Mother Goose, The Encyclopedia
of Tropical Fishes.

I grabbed a few of these,
shoved them down my pants,
so when he hit me,
he would hit the books.
But they only made it worse,
thumping hard against my thighs
and leaving Technicolor bruises
on my skinny hips.

I knew the books I read
would have a similar effect
because I never would
escape into a looking glass
or wardrobe, would have to wait
for years until I left.
And yet, these books
gave me instruction—how to live
a life where drama could be art
and pain might be allayed
by the very act of writing it all down.

A VALUABLE LESSON

by

FLORA GAUGG

The ability to spot a worthless item parading as a true antique was one that required much practice to be honed to the point that Prim had now proudly reached. And some fakes are ever so cunningly crafted. Even Prim was susceptible to the occasional, albeit rare, lapse in judgement.

In the days before her talent had been so rigorously sharpened, these lapses were of course more frequent. Many of them were here represented by the imposters that sat on Prim's card table in the cavernous hall: A rosewood clock that she had mistaken for an Atkins, Whiting & Co; an art deco figure whose tell-tale clumsy fingers evaded Prim at the time of purchase; a powder blue jug that she could have sworn was Wedgwood.

Each piece had taught Prim a valuable lesson, and for this she was grateful to each of them.

Nevertheless, she was eager to be rid of the deceptive little bastards.

In Prim's defence, some were really quite convincing. So much so that some of the less discriminating guests had already laid their designs on a number of them. Prim found it was usually the most unassuming characters who had the deepest pockets, and, unfortunately for Prim, the most discerning eye. Men in fine waistcoats and women with ornate brooches, she noticed, did the majority of the browsing and fondling and prevaricating, but usually left empty-handed.

And so, when an ordinary-looking man with slimy, dishevelled hair and worn corduroy trousers approached her table, Prim bristled with excitement at the challenge. Only someone stinking rich could be comfortable with looking so wretchedly poor. Pulling the wool over his eyes would surely pay handsome dividends.

When Prim greeted the man, he offered only a nod and a half-hearted 'morning'. Of course, Prim thought. Wealthy men are invariably laconic, except when they are very young or very old. Prim watched the man's face as he scanned the table in front of her. The only part of his face that moved was his brow, which lifted and lowered imperceptibly. Finally, the creature spoke.

'You've got some nice stuff here.' After Prim thanked him humbly, he added, 'too bad it's all bullshit.' Prim froze. She suddenly felt very exposed. She pulled her coat tight around her waist and folded her arms.

'I don't know what you're talking about,' she assured him, indignantly. 'This collection is very dear to me.'

'Don't worry, your secret's safe with me,' he whispered before floating over to the next stall. Prim hoped his comments had not been overheard by the neighbouring tables.

* * *

Later, when the packing up was underway, Prim described the enigmatic man to a fellow stall-holder.

'That's Jerome,' he told her. 'He comes every year. Accuses everyone of selling fakes. Given his...situation, none of us have the heart to kick him out.'

'Situation?' asked Prim.

'The poor bloke's destitute. Lives on the street. We figure what's the harm.'

* * *

Even Prim was susceptible to the occasional, albeit rare, lapse in judgement.

A QUIET HOUSE

by

MATT DIVERGILIIS

We'd really been through it. My wife Brittany's water broke early, she'd been bedridden for three weeks, and our daughter was born ten weeks early. It was like someone dumped happiness, sadness, terrifiedness, and holy shitness into an industrial-sized blender, plopped us in, and then flipped it on.

Now we were going home. I jammed the last of the stuffed animals into our Civic's trunk. I loaded in the flowers, balloons, and bags of clothing. There was no car seat in the back. *Don't say anything stupid* I said to myself over and over.

A few minutes earlier, the NICU nurse assured us the first time going home was hardest. "After that, it doesn't hurt so much. Honest truth," she said. "Call during the next changing time," she glanced at her watch, "about one a.m." We looked down at our Liliana, wrapped in a blanket, wires and hoses snaking around her and into her nose and throat and bellybutton. She was beautiful, a bit hairy, and just under three pounds. Our Lil Bear.

Brittany waited in a wheelchair under the hospital's overhang. I pulled the car around and helped her slide onto the passenger seat. She winced and pressed a hand to her new abdominal wound. "New parents aren't supposed to leave without their baby. This is unnatural," she said.

I didn't say anything. I didn't say anything stupid.

It was gray and drizzle blanketed the windshield, just enough to need the wipers, but not enough to keep them on. I manually flicked them on and off as we drove south on Route 18.

On. Don't say something stupid.

Off. Don't say something stupid.

On. God please keep me from being an idiot.

Finally we pulled into our driveway, got out of the car, and walked into our small house. It was dark. Our dogs Sandi and Patty greeted us with their wet noses. Brittany fished through her bag and pulled out a small white blanket, with blue and red stripes. "They need to smell the baby," she said and let them sniff.

We settled in. It was eleven and we wanted to stay awake until we could call and check on Lil.

"Can we watch something funny?" said Brittany. She propped herself up on our sectional.

"Sure. I'm making coffee," I said and walked into the kitchen. "You know," I said, "it's pretty quiet in here without a..."

You've got to be shitting me. Stop! Put it all back in your mouth, you fucking idiot. Too late.

"...without a baby." I doubled over and wailed uncontrollably. Brittany wept.

I slithered onto the couch. "I was trying so hard not to say anything dumb," I said, still crying. "I said the dumbest thing possible."

Brittany laughed through her tears. "What the hell is wrong with you?" she asked. We burst out laughing.

I made coffee twice more that night. Both times, I cried my eyes out then laughed my ass off.

BUCK AND BEAR

by

SARAH ANNE CHILDERS

Buck and Bear gobbled blackberry pie while they waited on the hippie. "Best in the world," Buck claimed between forkfuls. The flash of a red bandana at the restaurant's entrance snagged Buck's attention. He stood, wiped his mouth, told Bear to stay put.

The week before, in her sedan parked on the side of Scenic Route 112, the state game warden said Bear ought to get going. "You curious why the biotech guys pay so much for stolen bugs?" she asked. Bear didn't know about the payout because he took what Buck gave him, but he nodded and said yeah, he was real curious. "Because feral honeybees this far west don't get sick or abandon ship like the others. Control the healthy honeybees

– breed 'em, morph 'em – and you control pollination. As in, the food supply. It's true – a miracle." She frowned at Bear. "We could nail you for poaching on protected land. Eco-terrorists go away for a long time. But we don't want you; you don't know anything. Help us get to your pal, and we'll make things all right for you." Bear said he'd think about it, but already *all right* sounded better to him than *Buck and Bear* never *Bear and Buck* never *Just Bear*.

The hippie worked trail crew in the Olympics and moonlighted for Buck scouting bee trees. Buck had bought the hippie for next to nothing and laughed about it again as Bear navigated the truck to the trailhead according to the hippie's waggled directions.

They found the swarm shaking around its queen on a tall vine maple. Buck snarled that Bear was a moron for forgetting the helmets and ordered him to get his ass up there anyway. He did not watch Bear who sawed first the swarm's limb and then the thicker, heavier limb beneath it.

Bees shaken loose orbited the men's heads and attracted to the darkest spots, darted at the caverns of their eye sockets and nostrils. Buck swatted at his ears. "What's taking so damn long?" he demanded.

You'll see, Bear thought and grunting, shoved down on the lower limb to snap it loose and seizing it in massive hands, swung the wood to smash Buck in the temple. Buck fell next to the cardboard box Bear had pricked with air holes for the swarm.

The second hit knocked Buck out. The third one was just because.

Bear called the game warden from the restaurant's payphone. He left the vibrating box belted to the seat above Buck who lay bound on the truck's floor moaning through a rag, the goose egg on his head already purpling among welts that spread outward from puncture points.

The waitress said 'hey' to Buck and Bear before she noticed there was no Buck. Bear told her it was just Bear now because Buck was going away for a long time. She shrugged and took Bear's order for a slab of the world's best blackberry pie to stay and two pieces wrapped for the drive.

FUNNY THINGS ABOUT LIFE PART 47

by

ROBERT BEVERIDGE

little old lady
drives a big sedan
bumper sticker
on the back
"question authority"

TODAY'S WORKSHOP LEADER

by

ANNE E. WEISGERBER

"The prose has got to be," her hands undulate gently atop the very sea of air as her body sways, "rhapsodic."

Even when those sultry cabaret twins divide demurely to separate wings, her hands are like vaudeville comediennes circling like cranks of duel engines, "As you're... starting writing...," increasing strength to help the engines spit and catch, "...there's a certain dress... there's a certain cake... there's a certain something that's very Freudian... Themes," and then the frozen jazz-hands are left out, open-palmed fingers widespread, "...just come out!"

She taps to her ideas, "I'm not a fan of Moody's generally;" she's tapping on her invisible tabletop tack piano as she composes surface thoughts, "but *The Ice Storm*?" skimming octaves at fascinating speed and with strange variations, "come on!" Fiddles with rings: "He's an odd guy." Her elbows unstick from the podium momentarily, "This is literary fiction," those same concerto fingers hang over the table, "this is a story of human nature," rippling graceful and rapid, "of isolation!"

Hands explode away from each other to shrug, "and they are always eating meat in this book."

"I'm thinking," hands move toward face, "about hair," open fingers rippling, "the air," arms outstretched to make distant brackets, "and this scene where he's in a train," pulse-stretch wide for emphasis, "by himself in a train car," brackets closing, "with no power, stuck on the ice," closing further, "in the freezing winter." Hands are clasped. "It's like," now palms facing in prayer and moving forward and backward, "if you are in the true center of a sad onion, how can you not cry?"

Hands lift up like she's Trixie Friganza, that champagne songbird of long ago. Then, smoothing creaseless papers before her, "My pal Chekhov," patting the flat papers smooth, pushing the papers forward to clear the stage, "said it's time for writers to declare that they know nothing."

Fists sway-polling atop forearms, "You've got to," palms shock open with fingers splayed, "flame through." The left knuckle raps, "Why did you choose to write this story?" raps the right, "Why did your narrator choose to tell this story?" and so on knock knock knock, "Why is your world this world? What are you doing? What are you doing?"

Her tapping, tapping, tapping quietens.

"Listen: You do you." Holding a baton high, shaking it: "You run through that first draft like you're on fire."

Hands settle down, rest, steeple.

"Questions?"

THE NOBLE REGRESSION

by
RICHARD KING PERKINS II

Compensation for the wrongly dispossessed
is the greatest form of justice

and offers moral exculpation for those
who've illicitly derived benefit—

and so begins the noble regression to find
the people originally aggrieved;

a reversal of time trying to accurately see
the wrongs of the past through
the light of modernity

until we find there was a chieftain

in every community

who was outperformed
by a competing warlord just a little stronger
having wealth and subjects stolen

and we further witness
how those ancestral human beings

stole from the indigenous creatures of lowland
and forest

and how those beasts stole from the plants
and trees

which in turn had stolen valuables from the earth
itself

and we must reluctantly confess that reparations
are as illusory
as the need for sentience or vitality

that the planet doesn't care about the breathing
and in fact no lives matter at all

so that across the cosmos

justice is as irrelevant as age, temperature,
ownership, dimension.

SISTER

by

NOD GHOSH

My sister laces feathers through my hair and threads daisies around our wrists. In spring she shares black hellebore, winds spiders' silk through my fingers. We summon demons together, guided by separate truths. We are blessed as one in our wrongdoings.

We were conceived simultaneously, yet born years apart, my memories frozen before they had a chance to form. The coded clues for my existence lay dormant in a phial beside twin clusters, sisters and brothers destined never to enter the sanctuary of our mother's womb.

My sister is the older of two witches, the brighter of two stars. She wears her seniority like a cloak, decorated with seashells, pearls and the right answers to everything. She catches light in her sentences. We dive into pools of our mother's affection, compete for love, and come up wanting.

My sister is the icing in any celebration. She smothers me with wisdom, yet showers me with understanding. She claims the birthright of the elder twin, but protects me with the fierceness of a tigress.

When we are old, one of us will be without the other. The survivor will cast spells over ice and wait for the other to be reborn.

TRULY

by
ALAN WALOWITZ

Though it's not my way, I phoned to say I'm late.
Then I pull in haggard, out of breath,
and she uses her well-honed skill of indirection
to suggest I might take another look
at things I might not truly intend—my repressed
     hostility,
a certain passive aggressive tendency,
that desire to disengage, and with it
my failure to truly commit.

I tell her how truly sorry I am, and by it I mean
she couldn't possibly comprehend the traffic this
     hour,
how hard it is to leave the house
and not worry the wife and kids,
and my conspicuous need to mull any action,
whether complex or mundane,
while sitting in the driveway nursing a beer.

I could try the truth, but what if she won't hear?
Here I can be sullen or silent, even doze if I want.
She just rustles the insurance forms
that sound like crickets the hour before dawn.
I open my eyes to meet her earnest nod that says
she's working hard to think well of me
but is afraid our time is up.

I am truly, truly in love—
with the forgiving hours she's willing to keep,
that sigh as I reach for the door,
and her wan smile when I mumble—
and truly mean it this time,—
this time, I'm not coming back,
and her sweet voice that so truly replies,
Yes, but could you please try harder to be on time?

BOXING STUFF, ROUND 1

by

TOM SHEEHAN

Once, more than 70 years ago, I went 15 rounds with Bobby Lawrence in a ring in a garage that's long gone to dust. He's disappeared from my life, too, without a single clue. And once I fought Don Ryder in the same garage ring, but later, long after we had both served in Korea in our 20s, he looked over a co-worker's shoulder in an Alaskan pipeline camp, addressing an envelope to me, and asked, "Is that Tom Sheehan from Saugus, Mass?"

The night Sonny Liston fell down in Lewiston, Maine, I had innocently reached for a beer, a Schmidt's ale in a bottle that's gone forever, and the fight was over.

When Billie Conn went 13 rounds with Joe Lewis, in December of 1947, it was the same evening we tied for the national prep-school football championship at Manning Bowl in Lynn, MA against Admiral Bullis Academy from Silver Springs, Maryland, and later that night, in a small mansion, I was with a most memorable girl who was splendid at introductions to the new stuff of life.

When you talk about knockouts, it's true you're better off without gloves.

THE TRUE SINGAPORE

by

DUSTY-ANNE RHODES

On our most recent trip to the city-state of Singapore, where my husband and I travel frequently from Berlin as we build a business there, the taxi driver surprised us by asserting: "It's so great that you're here. We need you here, we need foreigners here. On our own we have nothing: no resources ..." Each time we visit we talk with expats and locals, collecting impressions. I asked the dark-skinned Indian driver whether he was born in Singapore: "Oh yes," his answer, "we've been here forever, my grandparents, their parents, ..."

* * *

Originally from Brisbane, Paul works in Singapore as an executive coach, supporting managers dealing with interpersonal challenges with their peers, their teams, their own managers. He met his partner Sing Lee when both were working in Hong Kong; after six years there, they moved together to Singapore, Sing Lee's hometown. "He's a B-level show star at the end of his career. In his last years on the stage, this is the only place it makes sense for us to be." Paul would love to spend part of the year in Australia, but his partner is not excited by the prospect. "To be honest, our communication is not very satisfying. I think it's a Chinese thing— never to talk about problems, just to keep it inside..."

He told me how it feels to be gay in a country where there's a law on the books prohibiting "act[s] of gross indecency with another male person." For decades the explanation has been that conservative Singapore society is not ready to be confronted with homosexuality. "I can't say I'm comfortable with it," Paul says. "There are state ministers, men high up, everyone knows they're gay. Apparently they're not actively prosecuting any more, but still ..."

* * *

I looked up Denise because she studied piano at the same conservatory in Ohio (graduating 18 years later). One evening she took us on a walk through the Tiong Bahru neighborhood. "These houses are some of the few buildings left from the 1930s. The government is constantly demolishing entire neighborhoods. No one in this city is living in the house they were born in. No neighborhood has stayed the same. There's a real 'legacy' movement—trying to reach back to earlier generations. Without continuity, it's hard for us to retain a sense of who we are. By the way: it's mostly expats who live in these houses now."

* * *

The city is always intensely green, always in bloom. The median strips have bright purple flowering bushes; the roads are lined with large trees, and you frequently see bucket trucks with workers trimming them back. We like to speculate how quickly the jungle would return were it not kept in check.

* * *

Mark shifted our first meeting, a breakfast, from 8 a.m. back to 7: "My wife has chosen the house she wants us to rent, just on the basis of some photos the real estate agent sent her. I'm supposed to go sign the contract first thing this morning—she wants us to move in next month. At 8:15, before today's meetings kick off."

Mark had been promoted at the multi-national corporation from country manager of Denmark to head of Asia-Pacific. At our second meeting many months later, Mark told us he spends most of his week pressuring and yelling at the 15 country heads who report to him. They look to him for stronger and more specific guidance about how to increase their revenue—and thus satisfy the big bosses back at headquarters in Germany.

* * *

When we're there, I read *Today*, a free English-language newspaper distributed in our apartment lobby and in many public places. I know it's not a properly researched and reported newspaper and that the media is censored, but I like to get a sense of local discussions, and of how the world looks from here: the possible significance of Chinese government policy decisions, tensions in the South China Sea, indignation about corruption in Malaysia, Myanmar as an "unspoiled" holiday destination.

The last time we were there, I discovered an article about shopping trolleys: "Last year, Fair Price lost 1,000 trolleys, each costing SGD 200 (approx. €130). The supermarket giant has spent more than SGD 150,000 on trolley replacements and repairs this year."

On the following day, there was a letter to the editor in reaction: "We have been brought up to keep our country as an orderly place so that all could thrive. I remember the national campaigns that exhorted citizens to do good: anti-littering, anti-smoking, speak Mandarin, courtesy, productivity, save water, get married early. Is our material well-being causing us to forget that each of us has a part to play in making Singapore a livable city?"

Aha, more national campaigns are needed like in the 1960s!

* * *

Siu (pronounced *Sue*; I observed that most locals of Chinese origin—74% of the country's population—have Western-sounding names they use when communicating in English) works as a wordsmith for a local telecommunications company, tailoring press releases and information material. "My grandparents immigrated from China ... but no, I can only work my magic with words in English! I am studying classical Chinese literature with a tutor though." We met through a mutual acquaintance: a few years earlier she'd fallen in love with a German she met at a friend's wedding, and she says, "We had to give it a try—it could have worked out—it seemed like we had potential. But I found living in Berlin without money just too hard. I did love it, though." The next time we meet over a bottle of wine, she shows me how Tinder works, handing over her cell phone and saying, "You decide. Just wipe the guy off the screen."

"But what if my taste is different from yours? What if I reject someone you'd think was wonderful? You're giving me a lot of responsibility!"

"It's fine, it doesn't matter. There are always more guys popping up on the display." The encounters with Siu, a self-proclaimed hedonist, could occur anywhere in the world.

* * *

Tom looks like an absent-minded professor—hair a bit wild, unshaven, wearing a yoga suit or shorts and T-shirt. Though we hoped he might suggest clients or projects after his decades working in Bangkok and Singapore, he warmed up most when discussing his self-published books on Heinrich Kleist (1777–1811): "I've figured out that no one has yet understood him properly. I'm the first to understand what he actually wanted to say!" He's the sole support for his Thai wife and their children, aged 12 and 15. The family likes being close to her relatives in Thailand; the kids attend an international school, at SGD 20,000-30,000 annual tuition for each. He hinted that the savings were dwindling as he pursued his literary passion ("I've been dipping into the family silver ..."), and that there'll be hell to pay once his wife finds out. Though he feels he's had enough of Asia and would like to return to Germany ("Berlin, of course, the only interesting city"), the rest of the family is satisfied just the way things are. He'll need to look for consulting work in southeast Asia again soon.

* * *

"I hate this climate!" Matthew told us. He was dressed in a short-sleeved polo shirt and khaki pants; we were in the air-conditioned lobby of the Singapore music conservatory where for the past ten years he has headed up the piano department. "I miss seasons. This here is just ridiculous!"

Proudly, he told us and the 20-odd students who were gathered that evening for a piano class, performing for each other, "I've now learned 16 words of Chinese!" He used two of them to describe the sounds he wanted his students to elicit on the keyboard. To judge from the laughs of encouragement his students gave him, as well as the refinements in their piano playing his words brought about, they meant "oomph" and "waves hitting the shore in a tsunami".

Afterwards, I asked him whether he always hams it up that way with his mostly Chinese-speaking students. Does he exaggerate because of language limitations? ("This part is really romantic, and I mean *really* ...") He looked back at me for a moment, then said: "The whole teaching process here doesn't function much using language. I can't talk about the differences between middle and late Beethoven and expect to get results. I'm trying to awaken raw emotion, to get to the source. And I'm trying to infuse these people with creativity— something they desperately need."

We walked to the road to hail two taxis. He lives just five minutes away, "but I always take a taxi. I hate getting my clothes sweaty, I hate that clammy feeling. I just hate this climate!"

A FICTIONAL ACCOUNT

by
LYNN WHITE

This story is fiction.
Made up.
Made up like a face.
First the base,
the foundation,
then the shadows and highlights,
the blushers and sparklers,
the reds and the blues
to add interest and shape.
Then lines for emphasis.
Black,
thick night-time black,
outlining the fiction.

So, there was a base
for this fantasy.
There was some foundation.
Even a made up story
has some links
with reality.
A spark from a dream,
an inspiration
from experience,
mine, or yours,

or someone else's.
Something written,
something sung.
A word, a phrase, a line
from someone's life,
their fantastic real life,
or imaginings.
becoming real,

becoming true
in the telling,
when the make-up
is removed
and the secrets
are revealed
between the lines.

OR DON'T TRADE

by

GWENDOLYN JOYCE MINTZ

I make it a point to avoid eye contact with people when using public transportation. I carry a book, a newspaper, a notebook and pen—anything to keep my attention distracted. On the bus or at a stop.

I was off from my restaurant job and had had enough of people for the day. I arrived at the bus stop and was pulling my book from my bag when a woman, who'd been sitting on the bench, asked about the upcoming bus.

She seemed nice enough so I didn't bury my face.

I was new to the city—I told her that—but I shared what little knowledge I had about the transit system.

116

We chatted further: Where we were originally from, what had brought us to Phoenix.

She had cancer and had come for an experimental medical treatment which had brought her a few additional years.

"I bet your family's happy," I offered.

She shook her head. "No husband, no kids."

She was quiet for a moment, then she shared her truth. "I had a fiancé but he died 17 years ago. My dad used to say to 'trade up or don't trade.' I never found anyone better."

I apologized if I was being nosy and then asked what he'd die from.

"Cancer," she told me with a chuckle. "Some days I find that funny," she said. "And sometimes I don't."

AUTHORS

Sylvia
AGUILAR-ZÉLENY

has an MFA in Creative Writing from The University of Texas, where she now teaches Fiction and Literary Translation. She is a bilingual auhor and has published *Gente Menuda* (1999), *No son Gente Como Uno* (2003), *Nenitas* (2013), *Señorita Ansiedad y Otras Manías* (2014), the novels *Una no habla de esto* (2007), *Todo Esto Es Yo*, and a LGBTQ Young Adult Series titled *Coming Out*.

David S. ATKINSON

is the author of *Apocalypse All the Time*, *Not Quite so Stories*, *The Garden of Good and Evil Pancakes*, and *Bones Buried in the Dirt*. He is a Staff Reader for *Digging Through The Fat* and his writing appears in *Bartleby Snopes*, *Literary Orphans*, *Atticus Review*, and others. Find his writing website at http://davidsatkinsonwriting.com/.

Danny P. BARBARE

grew up in The South where he has lived all his life. He has suffered from mental illness since he was fifteen and started writing poetry at the age of 21. He has appeared in numerous online and print journals over the past 35 years. He resides with his wife and family in Greenville, SC.

Paul BECKMAN

was one of the winners in the 2016 Best Small Fictions with his story *Healing Time*, and his 100 word story *Mom's Goodbye* was chosen as the winner of the 2016 Fiction Southeast Editor's Prize. His stories are widely published in print and online. Paul lives in Connecticut and earned his MFA from Bennington College. Find his published story website at www.paulbeckmanstories.com and his blog at www.pincusb.com.

Robert BEVERIDGE

makes noise at xterminal.bandcamp.com and writes poetry just outside Cleveland, OH. Recent appearances include *Chiron Review*, *Riverrun*, and *Third Wednesday*, among others.

Irene BUCKLER

taught in Australian primary schools for three decades, during which time she wrote many educational programs, stories for children and poetry, which have appeared in publications for children in the United Kingdom and in Australia. A flash fiction finalist in 2016's Hysteria (UK) and Field of Words Writing Competitions (South Australia), Irene's flash fiction stories may be found in various magazines and anthologies, in print and online.

Sarah Anne CHILDERS

is a writer, editor, and educator in Seattle in Washington State, USA. Her work has appeared in *The Drum, Six Hens, Portland Review,* and *Pure Slush* among other publications. Sarah is the Online Editor for *Lucia Journal.* When not scribbling at her kitchen table, Sarah can be found pedaling about on a cerulean bicycle with her daughter in tow. You can find more of her work at https://www.luciajournal.com/online-editor/.

Samuel COLE

lives in Woodbury, MN, where he finds work in special event/development management. He's a poet, flash fiction geek, and political essayist enthusiast. His work has appeared in many literary journals, and his first poetry collection, *Bereft and the Same-Sex Heart*, was published in October 2016 by Pski's Porch Publishing. He is also a prize-winning card maker and scrapbooker.

Danielle DAVIS

is a liar, a misremember of song lyrics, and a cheater at cards—only two of these are true. Her fantasy and sci-fi have most recently appeared in *Candlesticks and Daggers: An Anthology of Mixed-Genre Mysteries, Tailfins and Sealskins: An Anthology of Water Lore,* and *Andromeda Spaceways Inflight Magazine.* You can find out more about her work at www.literaryellymay.com.

Ruth Z. DEMING

writes from her home in Willow Grove, PA, a suburb of Philadelphia, in the good ole USA. Every morning, while her breakfast is cooling, she writes a poem and posts it on Facebook. Her work has been published in lit mags including *Creative Nonfiction, Mad Swirl, Literary Yard* and *Scarlet Leaf Review.* Before bed every night, she picks out one of the three or four books that are scattered on the "husband's side" of the bed to read herself to sleep. A psychotherapist, she runs New Directions Support Group for people with depression, bipolar disorder, and their loved ones. Her blog is www.ruthzdeming.blogspot.com.

Matt DEVIRGILLIS

enjoys life with his wife and two daughters in Point Pleasant, New Jersey. He has written and produced television shows for The Discovery Channel, TLC and Baby First Television. His short stories can be read on *Fictionaut, Istanbul Literary Review, 52/250 A Year of Flash* and mattdevirgiliis.wordpress.com.

Flora GAUGG

is a writer based in Adelaide, Australia. She has received recognition for both fiction and playwriting. She is interested in stories about ordinary people, and claims to be remarkably ordinary herself.

Nod GHOSH

works in a laboratory, has stories published in *Landfall, JAAM,* and various other New Zealand and overseas publications. Nod is associate editor for *Flash Frontier.* For further details, please visit http://www.nodghosh.com/about/.

Jack GRANATH

is a library director in Kansas. His poetry has appeared in *Poetry East, Rattle,* and *North American Review* among other journals and magazines. His website is www.jackgranath.com.

John GREY

is an Australian-born, US resident short story writer and poet. He has been published in numerous magazines including *Weird Tales*, *Christian Science Monitor*, *Greensboro Poetry Review*, *Agni*, *Poet Lore* and *Journal Of The American Medical Association* as well as the horror anthology *What Fears Become* and the science fiction anthology *Futuredaze*. He was the winner of the Rhysling Award for short genre poetry in 1999.

Lynn HOFFMAN

was born in Brooklyn and lives in Philadelphia. Among his 11 published books are *Radiation Days – a comedy about cancer*, *Short Course in Beer*, a very serious but tasty book about ales and lagers, and *Philadelphia Poems*. He is the founder of Drexel University's Culinary Arts program.

Mark HUDSON

is a writer poet artist, and he writes for truth serum, but he does not always tell the truth. Sometimes his perceptions are based on reality, and his own fantasy-like idea of what should be. He has always been a daydreamer, dreaming of being a writer, poet and an artist. Because of that, he struggled through school and every job he ever had, and has never been more content than now, being a "struggling artist." If not, it's back to fast food, or some such thing, and he doesn't want to learn how to make french fries, burn his hands, and have acne on his face again like an adolescent from the stress of fast food. He encourages everybody to find their muse!

AJ HUFFMAN

has had poetry, fiction, haiku, and photography appear in hundreds of national and international journals, including *Labletter, The James Dickey Review,* and *Offerta Speciale,* in which her work appeared in both English and Italian translation. She is also the founding editor of Kind of a Hurricane Press: www.kindofahurricanepress.com.

Em KÖNIG

is a queer poet/DJ/Winter Witch from Adelaide. Their work has featured in *On Dit, Flazeda, Uneven Floor,* et. al. They have participated in spoken word events as part of Feast Festival and in 2016 contributed work to the 'Queering The Museum' event at the South Australian Migration Museum. They were recently awarded the 2016 John Harvey Finlayson Prize for creative writing and the 2016 Sir Archibald Strong Memorial Prize for literature. Em is currently working on the collaborative music/performance/writing project *Climate of Cruelty* (www.climateofcruelty.com), which explores the links between the factory farming industry and the destruction of the environment.

Michael KONIK

is the best-selling author of many books, most recently the *The Termite Squad*, and a contributor to literary journals worldwide. His novel *Year 14* will be published in September 2017. In 2016, Konik was a winner of the Stratford Literary Festival's creative writing contest for poetry and the Barrelhouse Prize for fiction. A comprehensive archive of his provocative *Thought of the Week* essays may be enjoyed at MichaelKonik.com.

Len KUNTZ

is a writer from Washington State, an editor at the online magazine *Literary Orphans*, and the author of *I'm Not Supposed to be Here and Neither are You* out now from *Unknown Press*. You can find more of his work at lenkuntz.blogspot.com.

John LAMBREMONT, SR.

is a poet and writer from Baton Rouge, Louisiana, U.S.A. His poems have been published internationally in many reviews and anthologies, including *Pacific Review*, *The Minetta Review*, *Flint*

Hills Review, and *Clarion*, and he has been nominated for The Pushcart Prize. John's new full-length poetry volume, *The Moment Of Capture*, will be published in June 2017 by Lit Fest Press.

Michael MARROTTI

is an author from Pittsburgh, using words instead of violence to mitigate the suffering of life in a callous world of redundancy. His primary goal is to help other people. He considers poetry to be a form of philanthropy. When he's not writing, he's volunteering at the Light Of Life homeless shelter on a weekly basis. If you appreciate the man's work, please check out his book, *F.D.A. Approved Poetry*, available at Amazon.

Gwendolyn Joyce MINTZ

is an award-winning writer and a photographer. Her work has appeared in various journals and she is the author of two chapbooks, *Mother Love* and *Where I'll Be If I'm Not There*. She blogs at http://wwwonewriter.blogspot.com (infrequently).

Robbi NESTER

is the author of an ekphrastic chapbook, *Balance* (White Violet, 2012) and a collection of poems, *A Likely Story* (Moon Tide, 2014). She has also edited two anthologies, *The Liberal Media Made Me Do It!*

(Nine Toes, 2014) and *Over the Moon: Birds, Beasts, and Trees*, celebrating the photography of Beth Moon. Robbi has published poetry, essays, articles, reviews, and interviews in many journals and anthologies and on a number of blogs and websites. More of her work can be found here at http://www.robbinestger-poet-and-writer.com

Brian OBIRI-ASARE

is of Ghanaian heritage, and currently lives, breathes, works and sleeps in Sydney, where he happily inhabits an expansive world of language.

Carl 'Papa' PALMER

Carl "Papa" Palmer of Old Mill Road in Ridgeway, VA now lives in University Place, WA. He is retired military, retired FAA and now just plain retired without wristwatch, alarm clock or Facebook friend. Carl, president of The Tacoma Writers Club is a Pushcart Prize and Micro Award nominee. Google: Carl "Papa" Palmer to read more of his stories of poetry and prose. MOTTO: Long Weekends Forever

Richard King PERKINS II

is a state-sponsored advocate for residents in long-term care facilities. He lives in Crystal Lake, IL, with his wife, Vickie and daughter, Sage. He is a three-time Pushcart, Best of the Net and Best of the Web nominee whose work has appeared in more than a thousand publications including *The Louisiana Review, Plainsongs, Texas Review, Hawai'i Review, Roanoke Review, Sugar House Review* and *Wisconsin Review*.

Jim PHILIPPART

every now and then, writes some prose and poetry. Once in a while, some gets published. He sold his business in 2015 and, now, is learning to write. Contact him at timphilippart@gmail.com or visit his blog at imaginiscent.net.

Martin Jon PORTER

is a teacher who lives in Brunswick, Melbourne. His poetry has featured in Australian literary journals and magazines as well as the USA. His debut chapbook, *Traits*, was published by Ginninderra Press as part of its Picaro Poets series. A podcast interview about his work can be accessed via http://www.thebohemianbeat.com.au/radio/podcasts.html.

Stephen V. RAMEY

lives in beautiful New Castle, Pennsylvania, with his wife and two reformed feral cats. His work has appeared in many places, including *The Journal of Compressed Creative Arts*, *The Doctor T. J. Eckleburg Review*, and *Every Day Fiction*. His collection of (very) short fictions, *Glass Animals* (Pure Slush Books), is available wherever fine books are e-sold. For more information, go to www.stephenvramey.com, as well as facebook and twitter (@svramey).

Sally RENO

lives in a vaporish grotto where she serves as Pythoness to *Blink Ink Print* and Haruspex for *Shining Mountains Press*. Her fiction has been among the winners of National Public Radio's 3-Minute Fiction Contest, the *Moon Milk Review* Prosetry Contest, and has been nominated for the Pushcart Prize.

Dusty-Anne RHODES

is an American living in permanent European exile, mostly in Berlin. She originally trained and worked as a classical pianist, later moving on to translating, editing and communications consulting. Her first book consisting of 29 short prose pieces, *Hard*, was published by Pure Slush Books in 2013. Dusty-Anne has performed her autobiographical one-woman shows, combining piano and spoken word, in Berlin and San Francisco. Find her website at: http://dustyanne-rhodes.com.

Ruth Sabath
ROSENTHAL

is a New York City poet, well published in the U.S.A. and, also, internationally. In October 2006, her poem 'on yet another birthday' was nominated for a Pushcart prize. Ruth's books are *Facing Home* (a chapbook); *Facing Home & beyond*; *little, but by no means small*; *Food: Nature vs Nurture*; and *Gone, but Not Easily Forgotten*. The books are available from Amazon.com. Check out Ruth's website and her blog site: http://newyorkcitypoet.com and http://poetrybyruthsabathrosenthal.com

Barbara RUTH

writes at the convergence of Ashkenazi Jewish and Potowatomee, fat and yogi, disabled and neuroqueer, not this and not that. Her photography, memoirs, poems and fiction appear in the following anthologies published in 2015 and 2016: *Barking Sycamores: Best of the First Year; Yellow Chair Anthology; QDA: Queer Disability Anthology: Lunessence; Garland of the Goddess; Slim Volume: This Body I Live Inside; Spoon/Knife Reader.*

Wayne SCHEER

has been nominated for four Pushcart Prizes and a Best of the Net. He's published numerous stories, poems and essays in print and online, including *Revealing Moments*, a collection of flash stories (https://issuu.com/pearnoir/docs/revealing_mome nts). His short story, *Zen and the Art of House Painting*, has been made into a short film: https://vimeo.com/18491827. Wayne lives with his wife in the U.S.

Martin SHAW

quotes Elton John: "Born and raised a proper, I guess life just bugged him."

Tom SHEEHAN

has had 30 books published, with multiple work in *Rosebud, Linnet's Wings, Serving House Journal, Copperfield Review, Literary Orphans, Eastlit, Indiana Voices Journal, Frontier Tales, DM du Jour/Danse Macabre, Literally Stories, Provo Canyon Review, Literary Yard, Rope & Wire,* and *Green Silk Journal.* He has received 32 Pushcart nominations and been a Best of the Net winner. His latest books are *Swan River Daisy, Jehrico, The Cowboys,* and *Vigilantes East,* and he was *Danse Macabre's 2016* Writer-in-Residence.

M. Earl SMITH

is a native of Southeast Tennessee, and moved to Ohio at nineteen and, with success, reinvented himself as a writer after parting ways with his wife of eleven years. The proud father of two wonderful children, M. Earl studies creative writing and history at UPenn. When he's not studying, M. Earl splits time between Philadelphia, Cincinnati, and Chattanooga, with road trips to New York City, Wichita, Kansas, and Northampton, Massachusetts in between.

Vivian WAGNER

is an associate professor of English at Muskingum University in New Concord, Ohio. Her work has appeared in *McSweeney's Internet Tendency, Creative Nonfiction, The Rumpus, The Atlantic, Narratively*, and other publications. She's the author of a memoir, *Fiddle: One Woman, Four Strings, and 8,000 Miles of Music* (Citadel), and a poetry chapbook, *The Village* (forthcoming from Aldrich Press).

Alan WALOWITZ

has been published in various places on the web and off. He's proud to be a Contributing Editor at *Verse-Virtual*, an Online Community Journal of Poetry, and is employed as a teacher at Manhattanville College in Purchase, NY and St. John's University in his native borough of Queens, NY. Alan's chapbook, *Exactly Like Love*, was published by Osedax Press in 2016 and is now in its second printing.

Patricia WALSH

was born and raised in the parish of Mourneabbey, Co Cork, Ireland, and was educated in University College Cork, graduating with an MA in Archaeology in 2000. Her poetry collection *Continuity Errors*, was published in 2010, and her novel *The Quest for Lost Eire,* in 2014. She has since been published in a variety of print and online journals including *The Fractured Nuance; Revival Magazine; Ink Sweat and Tears; Drunk Monkeys; Hesterglock Press; Linnet's Wing, Narrator International,* and *The Evening Echo,* a local Cork newspaper. She was the featured artist for June 2015 in the *Rain Party Disaster Journal.*

Mercedes WEBB-PULLMAN

gained an MA in Creative Writing through the International Institute of Modern Letters (IIML) at Victoria University, Wellington, in 2011. Her work has appeared online and in print in New Zealand, Australia, Canada, USA, UK, Ireland, Spain, and Palestine, in *Turbine, 4th Floor, Pure Slush, Swamp,*

Scum, Reconfigurations, The Electronic Bridge, Otoliths, Connotations, The Red Room Company, Typewriter, Kind of a Hurricane Press, and *Cliterature,* among others, and in her books. She lives in Paekakariki, New Zealand.

Anne E. WEISGERBER

is a *Best of the Net, Best Small Fictions,* and *Pushcart Prize*-nominated author whose work can be found in literary journals like *Structo Magazine, SmokeLong Quarterly, The Collapsar, DIAGRAM,* and *Entropy.* Recent non-fiction appears in *The Alaska Star, Alternating Current, The Review Review,* and *Change Seven Magazine.* She reads fiction for *Pithead Chapel.* You can follow Anne on Twitter @aeweisgerber, or read more of her work on her website: http://anneweisgerber.com.

Lynn WHITE

lives in north Wales. Her work is influenced by issues of social justice and events, places and people she has known or imagined. She is especially interested in exploring the boundaries of dream, fantasy and reality. Her poem 'A Rose For Gaza' was shortlisted for the Theatre Cloud 'War Poetry for Today' competition 2014. This and many other poems have been widely published online and in print in some rather excellent publications. You can find more of her work on Facebook at:

https://www.facebook.com/pages/Lynn-White-Poetry/16036759832l3077?fref=ts and also at lynnwhitepoetry.blogspot.com.

Also from Truth Serum Press
http://truthserumpress.net/catalogue/

The Miracle of Small Things
by Guilie Castillo Oriard
978-1-925101-73-7 (paperback)
978-1-925101-74-4 (eBook)

The Miracle of Small Things beguiles the reader with a witty and compassionate portrait of a year in the life of Luis Villalobos in tropical Curaçao, where nothing is quite what it seems, and all can be lost or gained in a summer afternoon on the beach. Told deftly, with humor and insight into our very human vulnerabilities, this lovely novella by Guilie Castillo Oriard builds upon that quest for happiness we share, a sense of belonging, and makes me want to travel south to find my own miracle.

Also from Truth Serum Press

http://truthserumpress.net/catalogue/

La Ronde
by Townsend Walker
978-1-925101-64-5 (paperback)
978-1-925101-65-2 (eBook)

Try putting *La Ronde* down after you've begun to read – not possible. It sweeps you up into a beguiling tale of greed, mistaken identity, and desire. Townsend Walker has crafted a chilling novella with characters that pop off the page and events that will make you squirm ... a tale of greed and desire that will make you wonder ... what would your spouse do if he or she wanted to kill you?

Also from Truth Serum Press

http://truthserumpress.net/catalogue/

Based on True Stories
by Matt Potter
978-1-925101-75-1 (paperback)
978-1-925101-76-8 (eBook)

The small fictions in *Based on True Stories* will not lull you – they will piss you off or, at the least, move you to indignation, or tears, or laughter. Maybe all three. These gems provoke, like the tip of a chef's knife pricking skin, and just as the words get uncomfortable, the story delivers the bit of redemption that reveals the humanity of his characters – and of us all. These stories are real, raw, and honest. The reading doesn't get much better than that.

Also from Truth Serum Press

http://truthserumpress.net/catalogue/

Luck and Other Truths
by Richard Mark Glover
978-1-925101-77-5 (paperback)
978-1-925536-04-1 (eBook)

Richard Mark Glover spins larger-than-life tales of folks on the fringe in places where they tend to collect, with the focus on that great empty space known as Far West Texas. What might appear to outsiders as a whole bunch of harsh forbidding nothing – think Cormac McCarthy – these stories are filled with quirky characters brought to life by Glover's observant eye and quirk-spotting pen.

Also from Truth Serum Press

http://truthserumpress.net/catalogue/

Rain Check
by Levi Andrew Noe

978-1-925536-09-6 (paperback)
978-1-925536-10-2 (eBook)

Beautifully rendered, the stories in *Rain Check* could well be the footprints and photographs of our own lives if we'd have taken risks as daring as Noe's characters. Each misstep, triumph and regret rings true. Reading these stories is like being a lucky voyeur who happens upon an artist with brush in hand, nearing the finishing touch of their masterpiece. Nothing is more potent than prose that lifts off the page and lands, like a well-placed bullet or caress, on the heart, and that's precisely what Noe has done here.

Also from Truth Serum Press

http://truthserumpress.net/catalogue/

What Came Before
by Gay Degani
978-1-925536-05-8 (paperback)
978-1-925536-06-5 (eBook)

Five words scribbled on a discarded piece of paper ignite old memories for Abbie Palmer, leading to the explosive uncovering of a fifty-year-old mystery. *What Came Before*, Gay Degani's debut novel rumbles along at break-neck speed. I've long enjoyed the quirky characters and tightly-written plots of Ms. Degani's short stories and her novel didn't disappoint me. The book presents great characters, including a strong older-female protagonist and ably-managed twists and turns through the streets and people of modern-day Los Angeles, as well as the L.A. of 50 years ago. Old-school suspense at its best.

Also from Truth Serum Press

http://truthserumpress.net/catalogue/

happyme@t.us
by Kim Conklin
978-1-925536-07-2 (paperback)
978-1-925536-08-9 (eBook)

To be everywhere and nowhere, all at once ... Through her stories, Kim Conklin takes us on a journey of the human condition, where the everyday becomes foreign and dangerous, while the oddities of our world provide us with strange comfort. Each story is unsettling, passionate, thoughtful, provocative and reaffirming; taking the reader everywhere and nowhere, all at once. Dark tales, deftly told.

Also from Truth Serum Press
http://truthserumpress.net/catalogue/

Deer Michigan
by Jack C. Buck
978-1-925536-25-6 (paperback)
978-1-925536-26-3 (eBook)

"Something quite wonderful happens when you allow yourself to drift through life without a plan of direction," writes Jack Buck in his poignant debut story collection. *Deer Michigan* takes this heart, embracing the flux of fate in over fifty ethereal narratives. In one story we meet an exiled Mao on a hiking trail, in another the narrator mourns the graceful disappearance of birds. Buck's stories ripple with nostalgia, a reverence for the natural world and an America with room in which to wander. Though the stories in *Deer Michigan* are short, they bottle up an expanse of human experience, offering a stunning universe of feeling.

Also from Truth Serum Press
http://truthserumpress.net/catalogue/

Hello Berlin!
by Jason S. Andrews
978-1-925536-11-9 (paperback)
978-1-925536-12-6 (eBook)

Paul is an average Joe from London. He arrives in Berlin during the exciting noughties and discovers a world of free love, free afternoons and lofty literary pursuits. Clueless and curiously innocent, Paul steals the hearts of those around him, leading to anything but a tender love story. Fresh and honest.

www.ingramcontent.com/pod-product-compliance
Lightning Source LLC
Chambersburg PA
CBHW050824180626
46814CB00004B/1442